Genie
and the
Witch's Spells

ALICE LOW
Illustrated by Lady McCrady

BULLSEYE BOOKS
ALFRED A. KNOPF • NEW YORK

Remembering David,
who was proud of me
and vice versa

❖ Contents ❖

The Haunted House

I'll never forget that day when it all began. It was April 7th, and I was walking home from school with my best friend, Marcy.

I wasn't really walking—I was dragging along behind her, carrying a heavy load of school books. I had just gotten a D on my math homework, an F on my science report and a C minus on my history test.

"Hurry up, Genie!" Marcy called, doing a pirouette on the sidewalk. "I have to get home and get my ballet stuff for rehearsal."

"I can't," I said. "These books feel like lead. I wish I could throw them away."

"What's going on with you, anyway? You used to do okay in school."

"I don't know. I just don't listen, I guess. Suddenly, I can't stand math and science and history. I never loved them, but I got by in them. Oh well, girls don't need to be good at them."

"Says who?"

"Says my brother."

"He's a pain."

"I know. He hogs the conversation at dinner, and my parents just listen to *him*. They think he's so great, especially now that he's on the honor roll and was elected to student council *and* became a Mathlete. No point in even trying to compete with *him*. Who cares about facts and figures, anyway?"

"Well, you're still the best reader and writer in the sixth grade," Marcy said. "That was a really good story you wrote about witches and ghosts in *it*. Speaking of *it*, get ready to run. We're coming up to *it* now."

It was the deserted, broken-down house next to mine. Everyone said it was haunted. Children ran past it at top speed. Grownups walked a little faster. Joggers jogged by with an extra burst of speed, and cats arched their backs and hissed as they skittered by.

The gate was half open, as though someone had just gone in or out. Marcy swore she had seen a greenish light in the bay window one night. *I* was certain *I'd* seen a black cat in the upstairs window. And one night, I'd heard strange sing-song sounds coming from inside.

"I'm not really scared," I said. "I guess I almost *like* having *it* next door."

"Well, I *am* scared," said Marcy. She dashed past *it* calling, "Bye."

But I slowed down as I went by, feeling shivery inside. A good sort of shivery. I should have been *more* scared of *it* than

most people. Everyone says I'm a sensitive person, and that I feel things more deeply than most people. But somehow, I felt drawn to *it*, as though *it* had a special meaning for me.

I knew I ought to get home and do my homework, but instead I walked toward the black iron gate. I couldn't help myself. It felt like a magnet was pulling me—right to the prickly hedge on one side of the gate.

There was something caught in the bushes. Something orange.

I put down my books and started to reach for it.

Elmer Scutt sped by on his bicycle. When he was past the house, he stopped and called, "Hey, don't go near there."

"There's something in the bushes—a box or something."

"Don't touch it. The ghosts are probably trying to trick you. They'll catch you if you touch it. You'll stick to the bushes."

He rode off, and I tried to leave, too. But I couldn't.

I was pulled a step closer. Now I saw that the thing in the bushes was an orange notebook. Probably someone had thrown it out on clean-up day. Someone who lived in the house? But the house was deserted. Did ghosts have orange notebooks? Of course not! There weren't any ghosts in the house. It was just fun to imagine them.

I reached into the bushes. "Ugh!" I said. Something slithery! A snake? Or a frog?

I picked up a long stick and poked at the notebook. It fell down, but on the wrong side of the fence. Inside.

Now how could I get it without going *in*? I'd have to leave it. Even if there weren't ghosts in there, there were lots of snakes and spiders and frogs. Everyone said so. And the sign said, "No Trespassing."

I could see the writing on the cover, for the book had fallen face up.

"KOOB IM," it said in spidery, big black letters.

It's in a strange language, I thought. Really strange! I have to get it.

I ran home, got a rake from the tool shed and ran back. My heart was pounding—a little from fear, a little from running fast, but mostly from excitement.

I put the end of the rake over the fence. When the prongs touched the book, I pushed it along toward the gate. Carefully, I pulled the book through the gate toward me.

I picked up the book and opened it.

The first page had more scribbly writing that went uphill. Lots of words were crossed out, but the words I *could* read were in that strange language.

EEWOOF was written in the margins, over and over. What did that mean? There were ink blots on some words, blobs of red jam on others and lots of doodles.

I ran home, thinking the person who wrote this isn't much of a student. Probably gets bored in class just like I do.

But what class? And who was the person who wrote it?

I sat down under the apple tree on my front lawn and tried to decipher the words.

❖2❖

Breaking the Code

EEWOOF – what a strange word, I thought. I said it out loud. "EEWOOF." Dog language, maybe?

Then I turned to the next page. It had four lines that looked like this:

EMURB EMURB
EMUR IM ENELK ~~NEELK~~
EELKIWK TTI EUD
!EMUZ !PAZ !PIZ

It certainly *is* in code, I thought. But a really impossible one.

All the effort was making me hungry. I took the book into the kitchen, opened the refrigerator and took out a bowl of chocolate pudding. After I had finished it, I went up to my room and sat on my bed, studying the page.

It didn't mean a thing to me. I turned to the next page. This was how it looked:

Z RENNUR, ZREKWAW
GGOJ OOH ~~OOW~~ EZOHT
SSAP UNEW
GGORF A MUCEB

Weird!

My mother came home from work and said, "Hi, Genie. I'm beat. How was your day? Did you put the casserole in the oven?"

"Oh, I forgot," I said. "I'll do it now."

"No, don't bother. I don't want to interrupt your studying."

I felt guilty that she thought I was studying. But I could always stay up late and do my math homework.

10

She kept standing at my door, reading the mail. "Here's a letter from your teacher. I wonder what it could be." She opened it and read it quickly while I waited, feeling uncomfortable.

At last she said, "I can't believe it. She says you're doing poorly in math *and* science *and* history. What is going on with you?"

I just shrugged.

"Don't you have anything to say for yourself?"

I had plenty to say for myself—about how there was no use competing with Bill and how they gave him all their attention. But I didn't want to make it any worse for her. She looked so tired and discouraged.

So I said, "Bill says girls don't need to be good at those subjects."

"Well, you shouldn't listen to Bill."

"*You* do," I wanted to say, but I didn't.

She left. I'd think about my teacher's note later. Now I wanted to get on with breaking the code.

But I didn't get anywhere.

Bill hogged the conversation at dinner again. He was telling my parents about how he'd caught the math teacher making a mistake and how he had corrected him.

"I'll bet the math teacher was angry," said my father.

"Only a little," said Bill. "He likes me a lot."

"I don't blame him," said my father. "You're a whiz."

That made me think Bill could decode the writing in a second. But I wasn't going to ask him. This was *my* project.

". . . and we had a letter from Genie's teacher," my mother was telling my father. "She's having a lot of trouble in school."

They all looked at me. I was certainly getting attention, but the wrong kind. "I've had a bad week," I said. "I'll try to do better."

And I left the table and ran up to my room, crying.

After a while, I tried to pick up my math

book, but I kept dropping it. The reason was clear. I was not meant to do it now. I was meant to decode the words in the orange book.

"Math sharpens your mind," I could hear my teacher saying. Well, that was true of this orange book, too. It was a puzzle. If I could unravel it, it was bound to sharpen my mind. Ms. Haber would be proud of me if I did it!

But I couldn't. I kept going over and over it.

Then I noticed something. Some of the lines started with the same letters. I circled them, like this:

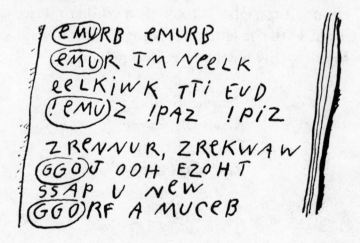

It *was* some sort of pattern. Could it be a rhyme pattern?

But rhymes should come at the end of a line, not the beginning.

Finally, I gave up and went to bed. But I couldn't sleep. EMU, EMU, GGO, GGO kept going around and around in my head.

Rhymes at the beginning, not the end of the line. That thought kept going around in my head, too. Should be at the end. Backwards! All backwards!

That was it!

I got up and switched on the light.

I held the book up to the mirror. Now the letters were backwards, but the writing went from left to right. It took me a while to write it out with the letters all going the right way. Finally, this is what I read out loud:

> *"Brume, Brume*
> *Kleen Mi Rume*
> *Due Itt Kwiklee*
> *Zip! Zap! Zume!"*

"Wow!" I said out loud. "This person not only writes backwards, but he or she can't spell, either."

Spell! That was it. It sounded like a witch's spell!

The next one, held up to the mirror, said:

> *"Wawkerz, Runnerz*
> *Thoze Hoo Jogg*
> *Wen U Pass*
> *Becum A Frogg."*

It *is* a spell, I thought. A spell against joggers. I was glad I didn't jog. I didn't want to become a frog.

Maybe the frogs and snakes crawling around *its* front yard had all been people once.

Now I knew for sure that a witch lived next door. All the people who had been scared were right. But I still didn't feel *really* scared.

And what did EEWOOF mean, anyway?

I held that page up to the mirror, too.

"*Foowee*," I said out loud.

That must be *phooey*. What kind of a witch would write *phooey* all over the place?

❖3❖

I Meet My Next-Door Neighbor

I got back into bed, repeating the rhymes or spells or whatever they were. I liked the sound of the words. "Zip! Zap! Zoom!" I said, over and over.

Every time I said them there was a buzzing in my ears, as if I had dialed someone on the phone and were waiting for them to answer. I couldn't go to sleep. Even when I *thought* the words Zip! Zap! Zoom! I still heard the buzzing, as though I'd made a connection.

17

I felt restless, too. I couldn't get into a comfortable position. No matter which way I lay, my arms and legs felt tingly, the way you feel when your foot is going to sleep. Except it was a more alive feeling than that.

So I sat up in bed and pretended I wasn't *trying* to go to sleep. I felt as though I were waiting for something to happen. Something good and exciting and something bad and scary, all mixed together.

I got up and looked out the window. That's when I saw the green light Marcy had seen in the window of *it*. I thought I saw a face, too, underneath the green light.

I ran back to bed and pulled the covers up to my chin. Then I lay on my back, waiting. I heard a whooshing noise, like a sudden wind, but louder. Maybe it's a tornado, I thought.

Then, BANG! What was that?

I sat up.

The old window had slammed shut. I'd forgotten to prop it up with a stick. But why were the curtains moving? With the window shut, there was no breeze to blow them.

I could hear the curtains rustling, and I could see them moving, even more now. And then, I saw that green light glowing through them on the right where there was a big bulge. I could hear breathing, too, as though someone were out of breath.

I should have run to my parents' room to get help. But I had that same feeling of being pulled, this time toward the curtains.

I walked calmly toward the window and said, "Whoever you are, come out!"

The curtains rustled again. Then, a shaky voice said, "It's me."

"Who?"

"Merlina—I'm a witch. But I can't come out. My cape is caught in the window."

"I'll fix that," I said. First, I had to pull open the curtains, slowly, so I wouldn't frighten Merlina. That was funny, me being afraid of frightening a witch. But she sounded so unsure of herself.

One last pull, and there she was in the moonlight. Her green pointed hat, glowing in the dark, was tipped to one side, and her purple and yellow plaid cape was torn where it had been caught. She was wearing sneakers, one red and one blue, and there were smudges of jam on her face. She was plump—no, chunky—and her hair was frizzy and red, sticking out in all directions. She didn't look at all like witches in books. She looked more like a clown.

I turned on the light, and she looked around my room. "Oh, good!" she said. "It's just as messy as mine, except much nicer. I live next door, but don't tell anyone. I'm not supposed to associate with humans."

"I won't," I said. "But I'm not surprised you're a witch. I sort of felt there was someone special living there. I've never been afraid when I go by. The others are."

"Good! I thought we'd bungled that haunted house bit like we bungle everything else we try to do."

"Who's we?"

"My mother and I. You see, we're illiterate. That means we can't read and write. Hardly, anyway."

"I know what it means, silly. I can't do math or science or history, but I can read and write very well."

"I know. I looked out the window and saw you reading my book. You read *my* writing, and nobody else can. I can't even read it myself."

"That's because you write your lines backwards. And messy. And your spelling is terrible!"

"I know. That's why I was kicked out of Witch School yesterday. I can't learn the spells because I can't read them."

"Maybe I can help you."

"I certainly hope so. That's the reason I came. After the teacher kicked me out of school, I threw my notebook away. Tossed it right out the window. And then I wished very hard that the right person would find it somehow."

22

"Am I the right person?"

"Yes. When I heard you chanting the spells, I knew for certain you were special, though you don't look it. You look very regular, with that dark wavy hair that stays in place. Very neat looking."

"I hate looking regular. When I meet someone new they always say I look like someone else they know. The only thing that makes me different is that I'm short for my age, and I don't like that, either. My father always says, 'Stand up straight. Then you'll be taller.' "

"At least you're not chubby like me. I love sweets. Especially jam. All by itself."

"I only like it with peanut butter. Let's see. Where were we? Oh, I know what I wanted to ask. What do they teach you at Witch School?"

"Spells, spells and more spells. It's really boring."

"Like learning multiplication tables."

"I guess so. But it's boring staying home, too. There's nobody to play with. All the other witches are at Witch School."

"Who else lives with you?"

"Nobody. There's just me and my mother."

"Why don't you live with the other witches?"

"We used to, but my mother likes doing things her own way. She has her own way of making brew, and she makes up her own spells. They hardly ever work, of course. She even refuses to dress like a witch. She hates black, and she wears the most outland-ish outfits. You should see her green glowing sneakers!"

"Oh, that's why *you're* dressed so oddly."

"Yes. She finds all my clothes in piles people throw away. Then she remakes them. And she loves to paint some of them with that paint that glows in the dark."

"Like your hat," I said.

"Yes. I look different enough from other witches without dressing like this."

"Did they kick you out of the place where

the other witches live?"

"The Witch Commune, you mean? I'm not sure. My mother says she left on her own to find a less conventional way of life. But I think she'd like to go back. Sometimes she looks like she's been crying."

"How long have you been next door?"

"About a year. That's the longest we've lived anywhere. Once, we lived in an old, leaky tent. After that, we lived in an abandoned railroad car. But the best place we ever lived was in the Witches' Tunnel Ride in the amusement park. That was our only success. We were great at scaring people there, night and day."

"Then why didn't you stay?"

"I guess my mother wanted me to lead a more regular life, without any distractions. She commutes to the amusement park, but she makes me stay home and study, so I can be readmitted to Witch School. I hate studying. I hate sitting still."

She flew around my room in fits and

starts, not fast like a witch should. And she was so clumsy she bumped into my lamp and knocked it over. She didn't pick it up, either. I had to.

She landed on my bed and said, "My mother is furious with me for being kicked out of Witch School, even though she was kicked out herself. She wants me to succeed where she failed."

"That's not fair of her."

"Well, parents aren't always fair, are they?"

"Mine used to be pretty decent, though they always paid more attention to my brother. But now that he's won lots of honors, they practically ignore me, except to pick on me because I'm doing badly in school. I'm afraid I'm going to flunk a few courses."

"Maybe *I* can help *you*. By saying spells."

"How? You don't know any."

"I would if you helped me learn them. I have a terrible memory. But I could say the quick-learning spells if you read them to me slowly, one line at a time. Then the answers you need in school will come to you, presto! You won't even have to think."

"But do witches have quick-learning spells for math and science and history?"

"Of course! That's how witches get through Witch School so quickly. What takes you twelve years only takes witches one. Except for me."

"Wow! But why not teach *me* the spells, and *I'll* say them?"

"Spells only work if witches say them. I'd have to say them right before each of your classes—sit next to you and be your right-hand person. Left-hand, I mean. I'm left-handed."

"That's impossible. They wouldn't let a witch into my school."

"But I could become invisible—there's a spell in my book for that. Or I could change into a frog, so I could fit in your pocket."

"Ugh!"

"Well, a snake or a lizard, if you'd rather."

"Double ugh! Invisible sounds better."

"You'd better think about it. It's an important decision. By the way, what's your name?"

"Genie. It's short for Regina."

"Oh, Genie. Like in Aladdin's Lamp. That's a good magic name, like mine. My name comes from Merlin. He was a famous wizard. I'd better get home now. I'll see you tomorrow."

"Where?"

"Oh, I'll find you. Good night."

And Merlina opened the window and flew right out.

❖4❖

Waiting for Merlina

The next morning I chanted spells in my room, but Merlina didn't show up. Maybe she'd forgotten about me. She did say she had a bad memory.

The doorbell rang.

I rushed downstairs and opened the door. It was Marcy. I had to get rid of her.

"Listen," I said. "I forgot to tell you I can't walk to school with you. I haven't finished my math homework."

"You sure do look worried," Marcy said.

"I am." What I was really worrying about right now was whether it was better for Merlina to be invisible, or to be a frog or a snake or a lizard. Frogs and snakes and lizards were creepy, but invisible might be creepy, too! I'd never be sure just where she was. Or whether she was there or not.

Suppose I got to depend on her, and then she forgot to show up before a test, when I really needed her. I really needed her now, for my math homework. Maybe I should go next door and wake her up. But I couldn't go barging into a witch's house, and the sign said, "No Trespassing."

"Look," I said to Marcy, "You'd better go. I'm waiting for someone who is late."

"Who? We don't walk to school with anyone else."

"It's my new turtle. I forgot to wake her up. I'm bringing her to school for the nature table." I'd just decided that Merlina should change into a turtle. A turtle wouldn't be creepy at all.

30

"Turtles don't need waking up," Marcy said. "You just bring them to school in a bowl."

"Yes, but I need time to get her food ready. And I have to clean the bowl. *Please* go without me. Between my math homework and my turtle I'll definitely be late."

"Okay. But hurry. Ms. Haber will be angry."

I ran upstairs and chanted another spell, hoping Merlina would come. But nothing happened. It was seven fifty-one, and school started at eight.

Three more minutes went by. Still no Merlina.

Then suddenly the room became very dark. I looked outside. Black clouds were rushing across the sky toward my window. There was a rumble of thunder, a flash of lightning and a huge downpour. Then there was more rumbling, so close it rattled my window.

I ran to the window and saw Merlina banging on it. I opened it, and Merlina flew

31

in, shaking the water off her hat and cape.

"Why didn't you come sooner? You're making me late."

"I can't come in daylight, silly. Witches only fly around in the dark. So I had to make a dark rain cloud. The spell for storms is basic. Even *I* remember that one. What's your decision?"

"I've decided that you should become a turtle. Is there a spell for changing a witch into a turtle?"

"I don't *think* so, but I'll try. I need a little time."

"But we don't *have* time!" I shouted. "Hurry!"

"Read me the spell about joggers turning into frogs," Merlina said, pointing to the orange notebook.

"But I don't *want* to take a frog to school."

"I know. Just read it."

I found the spell and read slowly:

> *"Walkers, runners,*
> *Those who jog,*
> *When you pass*
> *Become a frog."*

"Good!" said Merlina. "Now we have to change the word *frog* to *turtle*. And *turtle* has to rhyme with the second line. How about girdle?"

"That's not a rhyme," I said. "*Girtle* rhymes, but there's no such word." I went through the alphabet. "Birtle, Cirtle, Dirtle," and finally shouted, "myrtle."

"What's myrtle?"

"It's a plant that grows by our front walk. Myrtle—let's see. I've got it:

> '*Walkers, runners,*
> *In the myrtle,*
> *When you pass*
> *Become a turtle.*' "

"Good! Now we have to put *my* name in it, and I have to walk in the myrtle."

"You can't walk in my mother's myrtle. She'll have a fit. Hurry. Think of something else."

"Okay. Don't worry. I'll just skim over the myrtle."

We changed the spell, and Merlina flew out the window. She skimmed over the myrtle while I shouted the spell slowly, one line at a time.

Merlina kept forgetting the words, but finally she had said the whole spell, like this:

> *"Merlina witch,*
> *Walk in the myrtle,*
> *When you pass*
> *Become a turtle."*

I ran downstairs and out into the rain. Would the spell work? No Merlina! No turtle! I looked around. Everywhere.

Then I saw something behind the birch tree. Merlina was a very wet turtle in a plastic bowl. "Wow!" I shouted. "It worked. You even have your name written on your back."

"We did it," she said.

"Yes, but now it's two minutes *after* eight. I'll be really late, and I still haven't done my math homework. I was counting on your spell for that, and now there's no time."

"One thing at a time," Merlina the turtle said as we went back to my room. Her voice sounded the same, except I had to stoop down to hear her. "We'll have lots of time."

"How?"

"Find the spell about turning back the clock."

I flipped through the pages. "There's nothing about a clock. Oh, here's one about a wrist watch. No, *witch watch.*"

"That's it. What's your teacher's name?"

"Ms. Haber."

"Okay—read the spell and put in Ms. Haber's name."

I was getting very good at reading the backwards lines, without a mirror. I could even read the misspelled words—very fast:

> *"Witch watch on
> Ms. Haber's wrist,
> Time go backwards
> With a twist.*
>
> *Clocks and watches
> Everywhere,
> Give us all
> An hour to spare."*

Merlina repeated the words as I said them, one line at a time, a little faster than before.

There was a whirring sound on my wrist. When I looked at my watch it read seven o'clock. "We *do* have an hour to spare," I said. "Thanks, Merlina. And you're getting quicker at saying the spells, too."

"Thank you for reading my writing and teaching me the spells. Those are the very first spells I've ever worked. Except for the storm one."

"Now you have to say a math homework spell," I said.

"There will be plenty of time for that at school, before your class starts," she said.

"I want to do it *now*. I don't want to take any chances."

"I'm a little tired. I need a rest. Don't worry. You can count on me."

I had no choice. I *had* to count on her. "Okay, Merlina," I said. "You relax for a while."

But Merlina didn't answer. She was fast

asleep. Would she wake up when we got to school?

I started off, wondering if this whole thing was going to work out. Or was I just going to get myself into more of a mess at school?

❖ 5 ❖

The Quick-Learning Math Spell

I strolled to school in a light rain. I was holding Merlina in her bowl in one hand and my school books and the book of spells in the other. The books didn't feel heavy at all.

When I opened the door to my classroom, Ms. Haber was the only person there.

"Why Genie, you're so early!" she said. "What a nice surprise! And you have a turtle for our nature table. Put it right here." She moved a starfish and a piece of mica to make room on the table.

I put down the plastic bowl. Then I realized that Merlina would be too far away from my desk. I would have to *shout* the quick-learning spells to her so she could repeat them.

"Ms. Haber, I really think Merlina should be on my desk, for the first day anyway. She's not used to other people. She sort of clings to me."

"I think it's lovely that you feel so close to your turtle," said Ms. Haber. "You're such a sensitive child. But we can't change the rules. Any visiting pet must be on the nature table. You can comfort Merlina during recess time."

"But what if she wants comforting before that?"

"That's the best I can do, Genie. Now, have you done your math homework?"

"No, I haven't. That's why I came to school so early. I think I'll stand right here next to the nature table to do it." One thing at a time, Merlina had said.

"That's quite all right, until class starts. You have a half hour." Ms. Haber went to her desk at the front of the room.

I opened my math book to page 127. Addition of fractions. The problems looked hard.

Then I opened Merlina's notebook of spells to the quick-learning section. I found the spell for math.

I poked Merlina. She didn't move. She was still asleep. Now what was I going to do? I noticed she had some jam on her mouth. I'd better get that off before anyone noticed. A jam-eating turtle would cause suspicion.

"Really, Merlina," I whispered. "You *could* have wiped off the jam."

At the word "jam" she wriggled and said, "Jam? Where?" Had Ms. Haber heard her?

"On your mouth. Shh. You have to whisper."

"Okay," she whispered. The whisper sounded awfully loud. "But I'm hungry.

Did you bring any jam for me to eat?"

"I forgot to bring any food. But I'll get some at lunch in the cafeteria." At least I knew how to wake her up. Just say "jam."

"Whisper this math spell," I said, and I read her the quick-learning math spell, one line at a time.

She whispered it back, like this:

"Chicken leg and turkey gizzard,
Be a mathematics wizard."

I started doing the problems. Why, they weren't hard at all. But I was writing so fast I couldn't read my own writing. I had to start over.

This time I wrote more carefully, but still quickly, full of confidence. I could feel my mind working and really working very well. That was strange because Merlina had said I wouldn't have to think.

I finished and checked the answers. Then I waited a few minutes to hand in my homework. I didn't want Ms. Haber to think it odd that I'd done the problems so quickly.

"Finished already?" Ms. Haber said. "I'll correct your paper right now."

"Oh, I'm sure I got all of them right," I said and walked back to the nature table. I whispered to Merlina, "Thanks. I'll get a hundred."

"Oh, Genie," Ms. Haber called. "You have three wrong. I'll go over them with you." She showed me my mistakes. "But you did remarkably well for someone who has been struggling with math. You had three wrong out of the twenty-one problems. That's a B."

I should have been pleased, but I was angry at Merlina. The spell had worked, but not totally. Merlina wasn't a hundred percent reliable.

I ran over to the nature table to tell her so, but the class had started to arrive. Marcy ran up to me and said, "How did you get here ahead of me? Did you take the shortcut

44

through Donovan's yard? You know we're not supposed to—" The bell rang. I didn't have to answer.

Everyone ran to their desks and sat down, including me. Now how was I going to get back to Merlina so I could tell her the quick-learning history spell? I had to worry about that all through our first class, music.

❖ 6 ❖

Merlina and I Help Each Other

In music class we were rehearsing for *The Pirates of Penzance.* I loved the songs, but I couldn't keep my mind on them. In the middle of the policemen's chorus I heard a familiar shaky voice. Merlina was singing along with the boys. Nobody else seemed to notice. Maybe I was imagining it.

After music, we had history.

"We're going to have a surprise history quiz," Ms. Haber announced. "We went over the chapter about the Aztecs yesterday, so the facts are all fresh in your minds."

Everyone laughed nervously. I was nervous in a keyed-up way, more than I was worried. I'd figured out how to get to Merlina, so I could whisper the quick-learning history spell to her. I raised my hand and said, "May I be excused?" That meant I had to go to the bathroom.

"Yes, of course," Ms. Haber said. "But I'll have to start handing out the quizzes without you here. So don't be long."

I flipped through the orange notebook, memorized the quick-learning history spell and left for the bathroom. I didn't really need to go, so I stood in the hall for a minute. On the way back I stopped by the nature table and whispered to Merlina:

"Misty musty cobwebs, shoo!
Let history be clear to you."

Merlina whispered it back perfectly.

"Good girl!" I whispered. "You're really perking up." I went back to my desk, feeling confident, and read the quiz questions. Most of the questions were perfectly clear. My head didn't feel all misty and heavy the way history tests usually made me feel.

My problem with history tests was that I had to read the questions over and over because I was sure I wouldn't understand them. That took so long that I never finished the test, which meant I lost almost twenty-five points right away.

But this time I read each one carefully, just once or twice. A few of the questions were really confusing, and I didn't spend much time on them. I concentrated on the ones I could do. I didn't worry that Merlina wasn't a hundred percent reliable. I knew the spell was helping because I could feel the gears in my head running smoothly. I was glad I had to think, even though Merlina had said I wouldn't have to.

I finished the quiz with five minutes to

spare and started checking my answers.

"Time's up," Ms. Haber said. "Now, swap papers with your neighbor, and correct the papers while I read the answers."

I swapped papers with Andy. He had five wrong, and he was a history whiz. It must have been a really hard test.

When he gave mine back, I had four wrong. I'd done better than he had! Still, I was a little disappointed.

Ms. Haber collected the papers and glanced through them quickly. "Class, I'm afraid you haven't done very well."

We all groaned.

"But I don't think it's your fault. I must have made the quiz too hard. So anyone with two wrong gets an A, three wrong gets an A minus and four wrong gets a B plus."

That was me. Wow! Merlina must be getting better at saying the spells.

The bell rang, and it was time for science. The science teacher, Ms. Pappas, walked into our room. We were studying magnets.

"Now," said Ms. Pappas, "magnets attract some metals, we all know that from our toy magnets. But what other uses do magnets have?"

Kathy raised her hand.

"Yes, Kathy?"

"They are used in compasses."

"Right," said Ms. Pappas and she explained how they worked. I was feeling so good I was even getting interested in magnets, but I only heard part of the lecture because I was trying to get Merlina's attention. I had to whisper the quick-learning science spell to her somehow. I couldn't ask to be excused again. Not so soon. Everyone would laugh.

I memorized the quick-learning science spell and stared hard at Merlina. I thought she nodded back. At least she was awake and ready for the moment when I thought of a way. I tried to listen to Ms. Pappas and slumped down in my chair, hoping she wouldn't call on me.

She called on Laurie, Vicki and Steffi. They all got the answers right. So did Margie and Blaine.

"Wonderful," said Ms. Pappas. "Now we have time for one more question—about the history of magnets."

Only five more minutes of science class. I slumped lower in my chair.

"What were the very first magnets ever discovered, Genie?"

"Do you mind repeating the question?" I asked. I hoped the bell would ring before I had time to answer. I couldn't think. I stood up and turned toward the nature table. Then I mouthed the science spell. I hoped Merlina could lip read. But nothing happened.

"You don't have to stand up to answer," said Ms. Pappas. "What is that funny noise?"

Everyone looked over at the nature table. Merlina was jumping up and down in her bowl. Every time she jumped, the bowl moved closer to the edge of the table. Then, before I could get to her, the bowl landed on the floor. Merlina was on the floor on her back.

"It's my turtle," I said, running over and picking her up. I put her in the bowl and put the bowl back on the table.

Everyone was standing up, laughing and pointing. That gave me time to tell Merlina the science spell. She whispered:

"*Gold and silver,*
Iron ore.
You shall know
Your science lore."

Ms. Pappas was still waiting for an answer. And now I *knew* the answer. I felt as though I'd known it in the back of my mind, but my mind just hadn't been clear enough to let the answer come through. Now it was.

"Long ago," I said, "the first magnets were stones. They had a kind of iron ore in them, called magnetite. And the ancient people thought they were magic stones."

"Excellent, Genie. You told me even more than I had asked. But your turtle is really a character. I never knew turtles could jump. I'll have to do some research on them."

After science class came recess. I stayed in and talked to Merlina. "Thanks," I said. "You really used your head, thinking up a way to get me over to you. You're pretty smart."

Her green shell seemed to glow when I said that.

"It's funny, though," I went on. "I think I knew the answer even before you said 'iron ore.' Do you think just saying part of the spell works?"

53

"Absolutely not," said Merlina. "If that were true, they wouldn't have kicked me out of Witch School. I usually could say part of the spell. I just never could finish."

"Like me not finishing history tests. It felt good to finish. Thanks."

"It felt good finishing the spells. I think I've learned them all. When I put them to use, there's a reason to learn them. We never put them to work in Witch School."

"Maybe they wanted you to learn them first. You were too impatient."

"Maybe. Now, how about some jam?"

"Okay, everyone is coming in from recess for lunch. I'll bring some jam from the cafeteria."

I ran to the cafeteria and bought a peanut butter and jelly sandwich. Then I scraped off some of the jelly and fed it to Merlina on a plastic spoon.

"Umm, good!" She yawned and went to sleep.

That was just as well. I didn't need her any more today.

After school, Marcy and I walked home together, as usual. She wanted to carry Merlina (in her bowl), but I wouldn't let her. "You might drop her when you get into one of your giggling fits," I said.

"I wouldn't drop her," she said. "And anyway, what if I did? Turtles have hard shells."

"Merlina is special," I said.

"She doesn't look all that special to me," Marcy said. "Say, how come you did so well in school today?"

"My head felt clearer than usual." I couldn't let Marcy in on my secret. She's not too good at keeping secrets.

When we reached my house I said, "Well, I have to study for the math test."

"I'll come in, and we'll study together. We always do."

"I know," I said. "But I have to do something with Merlina first."

She gave me a hurt look and said, "Well, I certainly don't care. I'll go to Kathy's and study with her. She's smarter than you are, anyway." And she walked off without saying good-bye.

I took Merlina up to my room and said, "Jam!" and she woke up. Then I gave her a bath. She rolled around and played in it. "It feels so good," she said. "They turned off the water in our house because we can't pay the bills. We don't have any electricity, either. It's much nicer at your house. I'm so glad you're next door. I'm not lonely any more."

"Doesn't your mother wonder where you are during the day?" I said.

"Of course not! Witches sleep during the day. They have to. They're up all night. I'm not used to being awake during the day. That's probably why I fell asleep during your class."

"Well, you'd *better* get used to being awake during the day. I'll really need you tomorrow to say the quick-learning math spell. We're having a math test."

"I'll get some sleep tonight instead of

studying. My mother said she'll be out longer than usual. I have a hunch she's meeting her sister who is trying to get us readmitted to the Witch Commune."

"I hope you don't get in. What would I do without you?"

"Maybe I could fly over every day."

"I hope so. Listen, I'd like to come over and visit you. I've never seen a witch's house."

"It's full of cobwebs, and we have straw mattresses and a couple of rickety chairs. *Your* bed is really comfortable. And I like the cover on it."

"It's a patchwork quilt," I said. "But you didn't say when I could come over."

"You can't," said Merlina. She sounded sad. "I've already broken one rule, just being friends with you. If I let you come over and was found out, they'd never let us into the Witch Commune again."

"You're nice to help me out and take a chance."

"You've helped me, too. I can still remember the quick-learning spells. Now I'll have to say the spell to turn myself back into a witch. Read me that one about the myrtle, and we'll fool around with it and make it work backwards."

Fortunately, I had written that one down in her orange notebook. I read it to her, and she changed it, like this:

> *"Merlina turtle,*
> *Walk in the myrtle,*
> *Become a witch*
> *No more a turtle."*

Suddenly, the turtle was gone, and Merlina, the witch, was standing on my bed. She said the spell for a rainstorm, and a black cloud appeared outside my window.

She flew out the window with a whoosh, right into the cloud. I watched it float across to Merlina's house. Then I sat down to study for my math test. I didn't really need to, not with the quick-learning spell to rely on. But now that I was doing better at math, I liked it a little.

❖7❖

Merlina Enters In

The next morning, the dark cloud came racing toward my house. The thunder roared and the lightning flashed, and Merlina rapped on my window. Then she said the spell that turned her into a turtle. She knew it by heart. I didn't have to coach her.

She knew the quick-learning spells by heart, too. And she didn't fall asleep. She was interested in everything that was going on in class. Too interested.

In French class she learned the word

"*moi*," which meant "me." And whenever Monsieur Merceaux asked, "Who can answer this question?" Merlina whispered, *moi*.

"Who said *moi*?" he said each time.

"*Moi*," she whispered.

"Somebody is teasing me," he said. "I won't stand for it. I demand to know who keeps whispering *moi*. Identify yourself."

Nobody did. Then, from the bowl on the nature table came a distinct, "*Moi*."

Monsieur Merceaux walked over to the nature table and said, "Who said *moi*?"

I held my breath. Would Merlina give herself away? But this time there was no answer. That made him even angrier.

"Someone has been acting like a ventriloquist," he said. "Someone is making it *sound* like this turtle is speaking French."

Merlina kept quiet after that, but Monsieur Merceaux had a hard time for the rest of French class. Everyone was clowning around.

At the end of French class, he said, "To whom does this turtle belong?"

"*Moi*," I said. Everyone started to laugh again.

"Your turtle has caused no end of trouble," said Monsieur Merceaux. "You must see that it behaves. If it happens again in my class, I'll tell Ms. Haber about it, and she will expel your turtle from school."

During recess I told Merlina she had to behave or she would be kicked out of my school, too.

She was hurt. "You're mad at me, even though I've learned the quick-learning spells and said them right. You're doing really well. What would you do without me?"

"I couldn't do without you. It's fantastic. I'm getting everything right. The spells are working even better today. That's why I'm asking you to behave yourself. So you can stay. I need you."

But Merlina couldn't stay in the background. She liked school and wanted to do everything we did.

We were making sets for *The Pirates of Penzance*. I was painting the leaves of a tree. Ms. Haber said I could put Merlina (in her bowl) on the floor next to me. That way I could keep an eye on her.

I love painting. I love mixing the paints and getting my own special color. I mixed green and yellow together in a jar and made a yellow-green. "There," I said to Marcy, "now the leaves will look new and fresh, the way they do in spring."

"I hate this brown," said Marcy, who was painting the tree trunk. "I think I'll add some yellow."

"Don't," I said. "It will look awful, like mustard."

"I won't paint with this brown," said Marcy, who can be very stubborn. We fought about it, but finally she let me add some red, which made the brown look richer.

Then I dipped my brush in my yellow-green paint, looking forward to laying it on with smooth, silky strokes, but my brush hit something like a rock. And the rock was moving!

"Eek!" I yelled. "Merlina is in my paint. Help me get her out."

Marcy pulled out a dripping, yellow-green Merlina. Everybody stopped working and came over to look.

"How did she get in there?" said Ms. Haber. "You must have put her there."

"I didn't, honestly. I'm sorry, really I am."

"Ever since that turtle has come to school, you've changed. You've become a mischief-maker. Monsieur Merceaux told me about the trouble in French class. I may have to ask you to leave that turtle home, unless you and she behave."

"You're going to ruin everything," I whispered to Merlina as I put her back in her bowl. "Why did you do it?"

"I wanted to help you paint. And I wanted to be a lighter green, too."

"You are," I said. "But now stay in your bowl for the rest of the day. And don't forget the quick-learning spell for the math review."

"I won't," said Merlina.

She was good for the next hour. We were reviewing math for the test we were having in the afternoon. I was picked to go to the board and do percentages. I was sure Merlina had said the quick-learning spell, so I knew I could do the problems. Usually, I put the decimal point in the wrong place, like when I did ten percent of 100, I came out with 100. That was pretty stupid. But now my head was so clear I could really think about each step. I multiplied like this:

$$\begin{array}{r} 100 \\ \times .10 \\ \hline 1000 \end{array}$$

Then I moved the decimal point over *two* places and came out with 10.00. "Ten," I said.

"That's excellent, Genie," Ms. Haber said. "Suddenly, you're really taking hold in math. The same is true in history and in science, too, I hear. Very sudden, very unusual, but gratifying. If you do well on the math test this afternoon, you'll give me a lovely surprise!"

Good old Merlina, I thought. But I

thought something else, too. Did Ms. Haber think I was cheating? She'd said it was sudden and unusual. *Was* I cheating, using spells to do my work? I didn't think so. After all, I *was* learning, and that was the point of being in school.

❖8❖

Merlina Gets in a Jam

When it was time for lunch, I headed toward the nature table to tell Merlina I would bring her some jam. But Merlina was gone!

"Merlina's gone!" I said to Marcy. "Help me find her."

"I'll help you later," she said. "If we don't get on the lunch line now, all the chow mein will be gone."

"We can get peanut butter and jam sandwiches," I said, as we filed down the hall to the cafeteria. "There will be plenty of them left. Come on."

"You're acting all funny, ever since you got that turtle," she said. "You say peanut butter and *jam*, instead of jelly. And how come you don't care about chow mein all of a sudden?"

"I care more about Merlina. She may be getting into more trouble, and then she'll be kicked out of school."

"So what?" said Marcy. "You're all wrapped up in Merlina. It's stupid." She sounded as though she was jealous of Merlina. "And you didn't even thank me for taking Merlina out of the paint. I'll probably have yellow-green fingernails for the rest of my life."

Before I could say anything, she said, "Ugh! I just stepped in something. It's all sticky."

"Jam!" I said, looking down at the red spots on the floor. "It must be Merlina's doing."

69

There was a trail of jam spots starting from the kitchen. It branched off into the hall that led to the primary grade rooms. I turned the corner and followed the little red dots, which were in a zigzag pattern. There were spots on the wall every so often, too. The spots became smaller and smaller until there were no more. I had lost her trail.

I looked everywhere in the third grade room, which was empty. No Merlina. Then I looked all over the empty second grade room, too. She wasn't there either. I had to find her before the math test!

Suddenly, I heard a lot of noise. It was coming from the first grade room. I ran to the door and listened.

Two first graders were standing on their chairs, and the teacher was shouting, "Erica and Michael, sit down! Please sit down!"

"But I saw a monster!" shouted Erica. "It's red. I saw it when I was putting away my jacket. It's covered with blood."

"I heard it!" shouted Michael. "It's back there, behind the lockers."

"It cannot be a monster," said their teacher. "Monsters are big."

"It's a *little* monster," said Erica.

"I can hear it now," said Michael. "It goes tap, tap, tap."

Then the whole class started yelling and screaming, "A monster! A monster!"

The teacher shouted over them, "Quiet! Be quiet, so we can hear the monster." The class settled down.

"Now we'll listen," said the teacher. "When we don't hear anything, we'll know that Erica and Michael just have very lively imaginations."

There was no sound. Then suddenly, there was a tapping noise, every so often, like something being hit, lightly. *Tap! Tap! Tap!*

"There certainly *is* something in the locker area," said the teacher. "I'll go and see." The children started shouting again, but the teacher said loudly, "I'll only go if you are all absolutely quiet." The class became quiet again.

"I'll go," I said stepping into the room. "If you don't mind. I think I know what it is. Something I lost."

I led the way to the locker area, and she tiptoed behind me.

"There she is," I said. Merlina was crawling around on the floor, bumping into the lockers. She was covered with jam.

"What *is* it?" said the teacher.

"It's my turtle, Merlina. She must have gotten into some jam."

"What a strange turtle," said the teacher, and she went to tell the class that it was a turtle, covered with jam.

"Get the jam out of my eyes, please," Merlina whispered to me. "I can't see a thing."

I carried her over to the classroom sink, turned on the faucet and put her head under it. "Thanks," she whispered.

Then I washed her shell while the whole class crowded around, watching. They kept shouting, "Let me see! Let me see!"

The teacher asked me to leave Merlina there, but I said I couldn't. "I have to get her back for the math test." The teacher gave me a puzzled look as I raced out of the room carrying Merlina.

I put her in her bowl on the nature table and said, "Now stay right there. I'm going to get a peanut butter and jam sandwich. You almost made me miss lunch."

"Get some for me, too," she said.

"But you had yours. What happened?"

"I got hungry, so I crawled to the kitchen. There was an open jar of jam on the counter. I tipped it over and got into the jam. Then someone yelled, 'Eek!' and picked me up and threw me out in the hall."

"And nobody saw you in the hall?"

"I don't know. I couldn't see. All the classes must have been out for recess. And the kitchen workers must have been too rushed to follow me. Now please bring me some more jam."

"Oh, all right," I said. "But only if you promise not to leave your bowl. The math test starts in fifteen minutes."

"I promise," she said.

I ran to the cafeteria, grabbed a sandwich, paid for it and ran back. On the way out, I ran past Marcy who was sitting alone.

"I found Merlina," I said. "I'll tell you about it later."

"Tell me now, while I'm eating dessert. I hate eating alone."

"But I have to get back to her. I'm afraid

she'll wander away again if I don't get back
with her jam."

"Oh, who cares about Merlina? Who
needs her, anyway?"

"I do," I said, feeling rushed and panicky.
"I need her for the math test."

"For the math test? Why?"

"I just do," I said, realizing I'd made a
slip.

"Well, tell me why. You always tell me
everything, and all of a sudden you're keeping something to yourself. If you don't tell
me, I won't be your friend any more!"

I needed Marcy as a friend, but I needed
Merlina more right now. I couldn't tell
Marcy the truth. So I just said, "Tell you
later," and rushed back to Merlina.

Merlina was still there. I opened the sandwich, scraped some jam off with my finger
and fed it to her. Then I said, "Are you absolutely sure you remember the quick-learning math spell?"

"Of course," she said, sounding hurt. "I

said it this morning and you did fine."

"Yes," I said, feeling sorry that I'd doubted her. "I'm going to sit down and eat and collect myself from all that rushing around." I felt light-headed and sort of trembly.

I went to my seat and ate the sandwich. I sat there quietly for ten minutes. When it was time for the test, I felt fine. I was rested and confident.

The math test wasn't bad at all. There were twenty problems, all on percentages, and I remembered to move the decimal point over just as I had done at the blackboard. I knew I did well, and I felt happy and satisfied. And Merlina stayed quietly in her bowl until we were dismissed.

On my way out the door, Ms. Haber pulled me aside and said, "You did very well, Genie. You got one hundred percent."

"Great!" I said. "Thanks for correcting it."

"But I do have some bad news, too," she added.

"Not a note to my parents!" I cried. "Not after I got a hundred!"

"No, but you can't bring Merlina to school any more."

"Why not?" I said, even though I knew the answer.

"I heard about the trouble she caused in

the first grade today. I'm really sorry that I can't let her come back. She's a most unusual turtle."

"I know," I said.

I took Merlina home. She was fast asleep, so she didn't know about being expelled yet.

Marcy walked home with me, but she wouldn't talk.

"Merlina has been expelled," I said.

"Good!" she said.

"How can you say 'good'? I really need her in school."

"Why?" Marcy asked.

"I can't tell you. It's too complicated. But don't you want to hear *why* she's expelled? She did the craziest thing at lunchtime. . . ."

I told her all about it, but she pretended she couldn't hear me. She wouldn't answer. She wouldn't stop by for cookies, either. That was just as well. I had a lot to discuss with Merlina.

After Marcy left, I said, "Jam!" and Merlina woke up.

"Where am I?" she said.

"At my house. And you can't come to school any more. Ms. Haber heard about you disturbing the first grade."

"I wasn't disturbing them. They loved me."

"Well, that's beside the point."

"Darn it!" she said. "I really like school. I was learning things for the first time."

"And *I* was doing really well. I got a hundred on the math test. That was because you said the quick-learning math spell. You didn't forget it."

"I didn't forget it. But I didn't say it, either. I fell asleep."

"How could you do that to me?" I was really mad.

"I fell asleep on purpose. It was the only way I could stay out of trouble. You figured out the answers anyway, so don't be mad."

"That's true. Do you suppose the quick-learning spells are long-lasting?"

"They must be," Merlina said. She started to cry.

"Don't cry," I said. "I may need you again. And maybe they'll let you back into Witch School now that you know some of the spells. I could teach you the rest."

"Thanks. And can you teach me to write and spell them right, too?"

"Of course!" I said.

"Good!" She said the spell to turn herself back into a witch.

Then she flew home in a rain cloud, and I went upstairs to do some homework. I wasn't sure how long the long-lasting spells would last. And I was beginning to enjoy studying.

❖9❖

How Long Will the Long-Lasting Spells Last?

I went to school the next day without Merlina. I was glad I didn't have to worry about her getting me into trouble. And I still felt confident about my work in math and science and history. I knew the long-lasting spells would work for a while. But since I didn't know *how* long they'd work, I was really eager to make the most of them now.

I raised my hand to answer most of the questions in every class. I knew the answers.

It was a good feeling. Ms. Haber was so amazed at me that she called on me a lot. So did Ms. Pappas.

My mind was racing along, and I had to talk very fast to keep up with it.

"Slow down, Genie," Ms. Haber would say to me. "There's plenty of time." But I couldn't. How did I know how much time there was?

I studied every minute I could, even at recess. Marcy was disgusted with me. She called me a greasy grind. And she was mad when I said I couldn't play with her after school. I was too busy. On top of everything else, I was working on an anemometer for the science fair. That was a device to measure wind speed.

"Why can't we do it together?" she said.

"I just like doing my own thing," I answered. I had always done science projects with her because I felt I wasn't smart enough to do them alone.

At home, at the dinner table, my brother

couldn't get a word in. *I* was hogging the conversation, telling my parents everything I had done in school. They were amazed and delighted with my plans for the anemometer. It felt good to have their heads turned toward me, and to hear my parents say, "Genie, we're really proud of you."

My brother wasn't delighted, though. One night he said, "Do you know what you are? You're a know-it-all."

"Like you," I said. "You always thought *you* were the greatest. You never let me get a word in. You were a pain."

"Was I?" he said. I guess he really didn't know he'd been acting that way. But he wasn't mad at me for saying so. He was surprised. He gave it a lot of thought, and later he came to my room to apologize.

"I'll try to stop acting like a know-it-all if you say you'll stop acting like that, too," he said.

But I had to tell him I couldn't help the way I was acting. "I know I'm acting like a show-off, but it's like I'm under a spell."

"That's ridiculous," he said. "You're just too imaginative." He stalked off to his room.

Of course I liked feeling my mind working so well, but I was in a frenzy. I almost wished the long-lasting spells *would* wear off. But at the same time, I was afraid they would. It was exhausting to feel I had to use my mind every second. I couldn't calm down.

The only time I could relax was after I'd finished my homework, right before I went to bed. Merlina flew over every night, and I tutored her in writing and spelling. First I gave her some lined paper, so she wouldn't write uphill.

"Thanks," she said. "They don't have lined paper in Witch School."

I also made an "x" on the left-hand side of the paper, so she'd know that she should start writing from left to right.

"That should be easy to remember," she said. "I'm left-handed."

I gave her homework, lists of spelling words to memorize. She'd come back the next night and spell them correctly. That gave me a good feeling. "Maybe I'll be a teacher when I grow up," I said.

She still got blobs of sticky jam all over her paper, but I had a solution for that. "No more jam," I said.

"I never thought of that," Merlina said. "And I don't want to think about it. How can I live without jam? I know, I'll switch to peanut butter. Peanut butter wouldn't be as sticky, and it's not red."

"But you'll still have blobs of peanut butter on your papers. Did you ever think of washing your hands?"

"We don't have running water at home," she said. "But I *could* lick my fingers." And she did.

Merlina and I were both making progress. I kept up the pace all month, getting As and Bs in all subjects—on homework, papers and tests. The marks were nice to get, but not as important as the feeling of being on top of things and thinking clearly. The marks *were* important to my parents, though. They kept telling me how wonderful I was. And I liked that a lot.

But at the end of the month, my mother came to my room before dinner and stood at my door with a letter in her hand. My father was with her.

"Genie, this is a letter from the principal," she said.

"Oh?" I said. "What does he want?"

"He wants to see us—you, your father and me—in his office, Monday morning at eight."

"Does he say why?" I asked. "Does he say I've done something wrong?"

"No," said my father. "On the contrary, he says you've done something so right that—he sounds a bit puzzled. And he says it's an unusual matter, one that he wants to discuss in person."

"Maybe he thinks I'm cheating," I said.

"You've always been so honest, Genie," said my mother. "I don't believe you could change so suddenly. Although it *is* sudden—your interest and skill in math, science and history. What do you mean *cheating?*

Do you look at other people's answers during tests?"

"I'd never do that."

"Do you copy whole sentences out of the encyclopedia for your papers?" my father asked.

"Of course not. I wouldn't think of it."

"Does someone whisper answers in your ear?" said my mother.

"No, I get the answers myself." Though someone did whisper things, I thought.

"Then you're not cheating. Put that ridiculous idea out of your head," she said.

"It's just that I'm sort of under a spell."

"I'd say you're having a good spell," said my father.

"Still, I feel all funny inside," I said.

I continued to feel funny all weekend. I didn't play with Marcy. I worked on my anemometer. I studied. But I did it all in a dull, plodding way.

I even asked Merlina to put an end to the long-lasting spells, but she said, "I would if I could. But I don't know how. I never got to that in Witch School."

"I think it's time you got yourself back into Witch School," I said. "Both for your sake and mine." I sounded like Ms. Haber.

"Maybe you're right. I feel ready now. I think I'll apply for a readmittance permit right away. I'd better go home and study for the test."

❖10❖

We Talk to the Principal

The principal sat behind his big desk and stared at me through his rimless glasses. He smiled at me, trying to make me feel comfortable. But I couldn't smile back. My face felt stiff. I kept looking at the floor.

"Well," he said, in an over-jolly way, "let's get to the point. Briefly, the reason I've brought you all here is that Genie has made remarkable progress."

"Well, that's good news," said my father,

squeezing my hand. "In my day, when the principal wanted to see your parents, it was always *bad* news."

"We school administrators have loosened up a lot since those days," said the principal, chuckling.

"We've noticed a change in Genie," said my mother. "But we always knew she had it in her. We're very proud of her."

There was a knock on the door. "Oh, that must be the school psychologist, Dr. Berger," the principal said. She's very interested in Genie's case. Come in!" he called.

Case! I thought. Then they *do* think I've done something wrong. They know all about it. I felt like a weight was pressing against my chest.

"I'll let Dr. Berger take over and tell you what we think has happened," said the principal. He introduced Dr. Berger to me and my parents. I couldn't look at her either.

"Genie has overcome a learning block," said Dr. Berger. "You see, she always tested fairly high in math and science and history, but for some reason she thought she couldn't do well in them. Or pretended that she didn't care about them. Then something happened to change all that."

"Yes," I said, before *they* could accuse *me*. "It was a spell. A witch put a spell on me, so I could do the work I couldn't do before. So it was like I was cheating." That idea had been bothering me underneath all along. Now I let it all out. What a relief!

"Now, now," said the principal. "I know you're an imaginative girl with a love of making up stories. Always been tops in composition and reading. It's a charming way of putting it—under a spell."

"Yes," said Dr. Berger. "But I'd say it's just the opposite. The spell has been broken, allowing your natural learning ability to come pouring out."

I heard other phrases: "... a rock that was damming up the stream has been lifted ... something has given her confidence ... we're very interested in any information you have about her these past weeks . . . would help us to help others with learning problems. . . ."

"It was a spell," I kept saying, "and it *was* cheating," but they kept talking over me. They wouldn't listen.

I felt faint. My hands were so cold. I began to shiver, and my mother said, "Genie, you look so pale. Don't you feel well?"

"I want to go home," I answered. "Please, right away."

My father helped me up and thanked the principal and Dr. Berger, and we left.

All the way home in the car I kept saying, "Why doesn't anyone believe me? I *was* cheating. Merlina, the witch next door, said these quick-learning long-lasting spells. Only I don't know how long they'll last. . . ."

They kept saying, "Now, now, you're just a little upset. Maybe you've been working too hard—need a little rest."

I stopped trying to convince them. I realized how impossible it all sounded. And it was just as well they *didn't* believe me. They might send the police to evict Merlina and her mother.

My mother had to go to work. She had a report due for her market research job, so my father stayed home with me. He worked at his drafting board on plans for a hospital his firm was building.

"Can I get you some soup?" he'd say every hour or so. "Or some orange juice with a drop of cherry juice in it? That always made you feel better when you were little."

I'd shake my head and go back to sleep. Once he put a cold towel on my head.

I slept all day, off and on. Every time I woke up I could hear my father tiptoeing around and the stereo on low. He was listening to some opera. I heard the door slam when my mother came home. And I heard worried voices in the next room: "She keeps saying 'Merlina. Merlina would understand.

I want Merlina.' " Then I drifted off again.

When I woke up, it was dark. I waited for Merlina to come. It would feel so good to talk to her.

But she didn't come. Not that night or the next. And she couldn't come in the day when one of my parents was home. My mother stayed home with me the next day because I still felt weak and all funny in my stomach. I felt guilty making her miss work. But when I tried to get up the second morning, I couldn't face school. I might bump into the principal or Dr. Berger.

At three-thirty, the doorbell rang, and my mother answered it. It was Marcy. I could hear them talking downstairs. The only words I could make out were, "I brought Genie her homework."

Marcy ran up the stairs and gave me my homework. She said, "I'm sorry you don't feel well," but she said it politely, not as though she meant it. Then she just stood at the door.

"I don't have anything catching," I said.

"What's the matter with you, anyway?" she asked.

I couldn't tell her, even though I wanted to. She *would* believe me, and then she'd tell everyone, and everyone would know I had been cheating. And Merlina would be in trouble with the other witches, and she and her mother would never get readmitted to the Witch Commune. Unless they'd moved already. Maybe they had. Maybe that was why Merlina hadn't come.

"Oh," I said. "I have a terrible headache. I just can't talk now." I really *did* have a headache, just thinking about never seeing Merlina again.

"It's probably one of those viruses," Marcy said. "You look awfully pale. I really feel sorry for you." This time, she sounded more sincere. "I'm glad you have Merlina for company. Where *is* she, anyway?"

"She's gone," I said. "I don't know where she is."

"How awful! I *was* sort of jealous of her, you know. But now that she's gone, I know how you feel. Like when my puppy died."

"Yes," I said. "Would you put some ice in this ice bag?"

"Sure," she said. She really liked helping

people, especially me. I knew we were friends again.

My mother came up with the ice bag and said, "Marcy had to leave. She was late for ballet." Then she sat on my bed and said, "You know, I've really been out of touch with you lately. I've been working too hard. That's probably why I don't understand what's been going on with you. I wish I could help you, but I feel so helpless. I mean, I can't make any sense out of what you've been saying."

"Honestly, Mom, it has nothing to do with your working or being out of touch. This is something no one can help me with."

Then I said, "How would you feel if I went back to getting bad marks again?"

"Well, I'd be disappointed. You obviously have a good mind, and I like to see you using it. But I don't see why that should happen, now that you've gotten confidence in yourself."

"But if it did?"

"Well, I suppose a little backsliding would be normal, it's all part of growing up. It would probably only be temporary, though." She gave me a big hug and said, "Oh, I forgot to put the casserole in the oven."

After she left, I felt a little better. My mother really *did* care about me.

I sat up and did a little homework. I almost hoped I *wouldn't* be able to do the math problems. That would mean that the spells had worn off. I could go back to getting my bad marks, and everything would be normal again.

But I had no trouble doing the math. I was still under a spell, still cheating.

❖11❖

I Learn About the Quick-Learning Spells

The next day, both my parents went to work. They had to. I got up, did the dishes and watched some TV. Usually when I'm sick I love to read. But I didn't even feel like reading now. I went back to bed.

Suddenly, the sky clouded up. There was that familiar rumble of thunder and a ragged streak of lightning and then a downpour. I ran to the window and shouted, "Merlina! You're here! Why didn't you come before at night?"

After I let her in, she said, "I'm back at Witch School at night. And that's why I couldn't come. They let me in. They were really impressed with my writing and my French. They're adding spells in French to our program. It will come in handy if we ever fly to France."

"Good!" I said. But I didn't want to hear about her time at Witch School. "I have so much to tell you—"

But she cut me off. "I have a lot to tell you, too. You know those quick-learning spells?"

"That's what I want to tell you about. Nobody believes me—not the principal or Dr. Berger or—"

"They were right not to believe you."

"What do you mean? How can you say that?"

"Those spells never worked. I just found out at Witch School. I made a mistake. I forgot to put your name in them, so they didn't work. You have to say the person's name when you use them on someone else. You

103

did all the quick-learning yourself."

"But how? How could I? I have a learning block in math and science and history. Dr. Berger said so." And I told her about the conversation in the principal's office.

"I guess the spells gave you confidence. When I said the spells, you thought you could do the work. So you did!"

"So I wasn't cheating, and I got the right answers all on my own!" I said. "Oh, Merlina. I feel so good." I started to get dressed.

"So do I," said Merlina. "Just a little sleepy. Witch School is really hard work. But I love it. We're practicing the spells now."

"I'm going to school," I announced. I picked up my school books, and there was Merlina's orange notebook underneath.

"I forgot to give this back," I said.

"Oh, keep it. They gave me a new one at Witch School, so I could make a fresh start. Look!" She opened her new book. "Lined pages. I made the lines myself with a ruler. Now all the other witches are doing it, too."

104

The pages were very neat. The writing went from left to right in a straight line. The spelling was almost perfect.

"But there are still a few spots of jam on them," I said.

"Oh well," Merlina said. "One thing at a time. I don't have any jam on my face though."

"No, and you sewed your cape." Then I thought of something. "Will you keep coming over, even though you don't need me anymore?"

"I can't," she said. "This is the last time. I can't break the rules anymore, now that I'm in Witch School again."

"But if I ever need you again?" I said.

"If you really need me, I'll know it and figure out a way to come. Wherever I am. But you won't need me. You can solve your own problems now."

"Does that mean you're moving?"

"Soon," she said. "We've been readmitted to the Witch Commune, but I can't tell you where it is."

"Oh, Merlina," I said. "I'll never forget you."

And I haven't. Things are back to normal again, only better. I study a lot more, but I don't get all keyed-up about it. I'm doing well at school. I'm working on a project for the science fair, and I still write lots of stories. I have plenty of time to play with Marcy and a new girl next door, Penny. We walk to school and back together, and when we pass *it* we don't run by. We go in because it's Penny's house now. It's painted yellow, and the fence is painted white. And there's a lawn in front where we play baseball and Frisbee.

It's hard to believe that it was once a haunted house and that Merlina lived there. Sometimes I wonder if she was real or if I made her up.

But I still have her orange notebook in the bottom of my dresser drawer. I haven't shown it to anyone, not even Marcy. For now, I just like keeping Merlina, the witch, to myself. I feel all warm inside when I think about her. Some day, maybe I'll tell my children stories about her, and I'll bet *they* won't believe me either. Even when I show them the orange notebook.

ALICE LOW is the author of more than a dozen books for young readers, ranging from picture books to novels. Born in New York City and a graduate of Smith College, Ms. Low currently resides in Briarcliff Manor, New York.